Isla OF ADVENTURE

STARRY, STARRY GHOST

by Dela Costa   illustrated by Ana Sebastián

LITTLE SIMON

New York London Toronto Sydney New Delhi

This book is a work of fiction. Any references to historical events, real people, or real places are used fictitiously. Other names, characters, places, and events are products of the author's imagination, and any resemblance to actual events or places or persons, living or dead, is entirely coincidental.

LITTLE SIMON

An imprint of Simon & Schuster Children's Publishing Division
1230 Avenue of the Americas, New York, New York 10020
First Little Simon paperback edition July 2023
Copyright © 2023 by Simon & Schuster, Inc.
All rights reserved, including the right of reproduction in whole or in part in any form.
LITTLE SIMON is a registered trademark of Simon & Schuster, Inc., and associated colophon is a trademark of Simon & Schuster, Inc. For information about special discounts for bulk purchases, please contact Simon & Schuster Special Sales at 1-866-506-1949 or business@simonandschuster.com.
The Simon & Schuster Speakers Bureau can bring authors to your live event. For more information or to book an event contact the Simon & Schuster Speakers Bureau at 1-866-248-3049 or visit our website at www.simonspeakers.com.
Series designed by Laura Roode.
Book designed by Laura Roode. The text of this book was set in Congenial.
Manufactured in the United States of America 0623 LAK
2 4 6 8 10 9 7 5 3 1
Cataloging-in-Publication Data is available for this title from the Library of Congress.
ISBN 978-1-6659-3175-5 (hc)
ISBN 978-1-6659-3174-8 (pbk)
ISBN 978-1-6659-3176-2 (ebook)

Contents

SNAIL
MAIL

◆◇◆◇◆◇◆◇◆◇◆◇◆

"Isla, you've got snail mail!"

Isla Verde looked up from her desk. She was in the middle of reading about different leaves on the island of Sol. There were so many types of plants that Isla thought the island secretly made space for more to grow.

Putting the book down, Isla swirled around in her desk chair.

"You're always a welcome break, Mama," Isla said. "I wonder if it's my new magnifying glass."

"I don't think it would fit in this." Mama placed two envelopes on Isla's desk. "One for you and one for Fitz. Take a look while I finish making lunch."

As Mama left, Isla's gecko best friend leaped up from his nap. "Mail from snails is the worst! Remember that one time we brought them apples, and they sent us back an envelope full of leftovers?"

Isla shivered. How could she forget the soggy envelope? "Those leftover apples had seen better days. But I don't think Mama meant *that* kind of snail mail. These letters were delivered by someone on foot."

Fitz sniffed the air. "These don't *smell* like old apples. . . ."

They studied the envelopes. One was bright pink and had Isla's name written on it in big, glittery letters.

The other one was much smaller and had Fitz's name spelled out with stickers.

"Who would send us such bright, glittery envelopes?" Isla asked, winking at Fitz.

"I'm no detective," Fitz replied. "But I think I know who they're from. . . ."

At the same time, they exclaimed, "Tora!"

"Let's open them!" Fitz said.

Isla opened his first and then hers. Even more glitter spilled out from inside the envelopes as they took out invitations. They read:

You are invited to
the ultimate sleepover costume
EXTRAVAGANZA

WHERE: the Rosa house
(next door!)

WHEN: Tonight! EEEEEP!

BRING: Fun PJs and yourself, please!

Fitz whistled, shaking some glitter off his feet. "She sure knows how to sell a party. Even though I don't know what an *eggs*-tra-va-gan-za is . . . do you?"

Isla spelled it out for him on a piece of paper. "It's *ex*-tra-va-gan-za. It means a huge party!"

Fitz tapped his chin. "So, there *won't* be any eggs involved?"

"Unfortunately, no," Isla said. "At least, I don't think so."

Isla had never been invited to a sleepover before. Not unless you counted the night she tried sleeping outside with the fireflies. Fireflies liked to put on light shows. She'd tried to stay out as late as possible, but Mama thought it was better for Isla to sleep in her own bed.

"Now that's a lot of sparkle!" Mama popped back into Isla's room.

"We're invited to the biggest party of the year! No big deal." Isla waved a hand as if it were nothing.

"Do you think this party could use a fresh batch of *quesitos*?" Mama pulled a plate of her famous twisted pastries from behind her back.

"Did you say . . . *quesitos*?" Fitz nearly floated into the air as he drooled. "Perfectly glazed, beautifully crunchy, and sweetly flaky?"

The mouthwatering scent swirled around them.

"Oh yeah." Isla sighed dreamily. "There's nothing like sugar to bring people together."

"I'll take that as a yes." Mama winked.

SOMETHING
TO WEAR

◆◆◆◆◆◆◆◆◆◆◆◆◆

Tora's invitation said that all Isla needed to bring was herself and fun pajamas.

The first part was easy. They were neighbors, after all.

But fun pajamas? Isla wasn't sure she had anything in her closet that was Tora-level fun. Where Isla thought mud stains were a sign of a day well spent, she knew Tora wouldn't consider that to be fabulous.

Isla paced in front of her closet. "I have good news and bad news."

Fitz watched from the nightstand. "I think I'll take the good news first, please. That way, we start off strong!"

"You're a very smart gecko," Isla replied. "The good news is that the walk to Tora's is less than a whole minute."

"Easy for a long-legged human to say," Fitz huffed. "But go on."

Isla pulled open her closet doors and cried out, "The bad news is that I don't own anything glittery!"

A couple of stuffed animals tumbled

down from a shelf. Then some vines twirled down from somewhere else.

"Huh." Isla poked the leaves. "I didn't even know something was growing in here. Nature really is amazing."

Fitz looked at all the things in Isla's closet. "I'm sure you have *something*."

They searched together. There was clothing meant for getting messy, hand-me-downs, and even a few old snacks that weren't Isla's.

She dangled a banana peel between two fingers. "This isn't mine, is it?"

Fitz chuckled nervously. "I was storing that for the winter."

After a few minutes of digging, they sat on the floor next to piles of clothes.

"I vote for shoving all of this under the bed," Fitz said, pointing with his tail. "We can't have a clear mind with this mess around us."

Isla followed the direction of Fitz's tail point. There, under the bed, she noticed something she'd forgotten. "Wait! I think there's hope after all, you brilliant gecko!"

She hopped over Fitz and reached under her bed. With one mighty tug, Isla pulled out a small trunk.

"What's that dusty old thing?" Fitz asked, letting out a sneeze.

"It has my old costumes in it." Isla popped open the lid. "I can't believe I forgot about this!"

"You mean we made this mess for nothing?" Fitz groaned.

"I wouldn't say that," Isla replied. "Now we get to put on a fashion show."

"Now you're talking!" Fitz said.

First, Isla tried on a pirate outfit.
"Argh, matey! What about this one?"

Fitz shook his head. "Not the treasure
we're looking for. Next!"

Next, Isla tried on a very round, very yellow bee costume. "Here's a honey-sweet look. Buzz, buzz!"

Fitz yawned. "You're buzzing me to sleep."

Isla then became an astronaut. Then a race car driver. There was even one costume that made Isla look like a cupcake.

"I have a feeling you'll like this one," Isla called out. She hopped out from behind a dresser, hands on her hips. "Ta-da!"

"Oh . . . my . . . gecko." Fitz clapped.

Isla wore an orange onesie fashioned to look like a gecko!

"Some of the scales have glitter." Isla wiggled around to show off the sparkly scales that ran along the back.

Fitz posed alongside her. "Wear that to Tora's sleepover, and you'll be the coolest gecko there! Besides me, of course."

"Best geckos for life!" Isla and Fitz did a fist bump.

Isla smiled at herself in her mirror. Now that she had the perfect outfit, nothing could go wrong.

ONE MORE SURPRISE

◆◆◆◆◆◆◆◆◆◆◆◆◆◆

Ding-dong!

"I love doing that," Fitz said. He pressed the doorbell to the Rosas' door a few more times.

"You do it well, good sir." Isla held the tray of *quesitos* in her hands. "Let's not break it, though."

Fitz stood straight on Isla's shoulder just as the door flung open.

Out came the one and only, the queen of pink, the empress of glitter . . . Tora Rosa! As always, Isla's newest friend and neighbor was dressed from head to toe in pink—this time in a ballerina costume.

"Whoa!" Isla said. "Those are the coolest pajamas I've ever seen!"

"You both look gecko-tastic!" Tora squealed. "That pastry tray looks *delicious*. It will go perfectly on our dessert table."

"Dessert *table*?" Fitz asked. "Did I hear that right?"

"I think you've got this gecko's attention." Isla laughed.

Tora led the way inside and into the living room.

The Rosas had gone all out for the special sleepover extravaganza. There were balloons, streamers, confetti, and music playing from multiple speakers. The dinner table was covered with a pink tablecloth and had all sorts of delicious, sugary treats on it.

"Where did all of this come from?" Isla gasped. She placed her tray next to a stand with very glittery cupcakes.

"Dad and I baked most of the things here. That glitter? It's the special kind you can eat," Tora said proudly. "But we also placed an order with Señora Honey over at the market bakery."

"Señora Honey is the best!" Isla agreed. "She can whip up just about anything in minutes."

"Come on, the tour's not over yet!" Tora showed Isla the theater room where they'd be watching movies, then the kitchen with boxes of pizza, and the backyard with a fire pit to roast s'mores.

Isla was very impressed.

"There's one more surprise!" T sang.

"I sure hope it's another dess table," Fitz said dreamily.

"She's upstairs in my room." T motioned for them to follow.

Isla and Fitz looked at each ot

She?

PRINCESS ELLA

◊◊◊◊◊◊◊◊◊◊◊◊◊

Isla and Fitz followed Tora to her bedroom.

The Rosas' hallway was lined with lots of family pictures. Tora, of course, was in the center of them all. She really, *really* liked photo shoots.

"I'm excited to see your room for the first time," Isla said. "If it's anything like you, I'm sure it'll be very—"

"Behold!" Tora pushed open her bedroom door.

"Pink," Isla finished. Her mouth dropped open.

Stepping into Tora's bedroom was like stepping into the pages of a fairytale book. Strings of twinkling lights hung from the corners of the room. There was a vanity with lots of bows, a table stacked with fashion magazines, and a rack with plenty of poufy dresses.

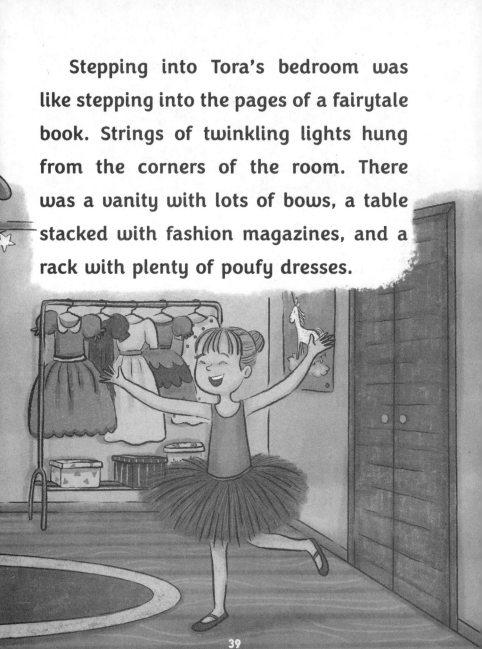

Isla's bedroom smelled like earth, like Sol. Tora's smelled like a rose garden.

"It's like the color pink exploded in here," Fitz whispered.

Suddenly, a flash of purple made Isla jump. "You must be the famous Isla Verde!"

A girl ran out of Tora's large closet and shook Isla's hand excitedly. "I'm Ella Louise Garcia, but you can call me Ella. I was just picking a tiara from Tora's closet. What do you think?"

Tora led the way inside and into the living room.

The Rosas had gone all out for the special sleepover extravaganza. There were balloons, streamers, confetti, and music playing from multiple speakers. The dinner table was covered with a pink tablecloth and had all sorts of delicious, sugary treats on it.

"Where did all of this come from?" Isla gasped. She placed her tray next to a stand with very glittery cupcakes.

"Dad and I baked most of the things here. That glitter? It's the special kind you can eat," Tora said proudly. "But we also placed an order with Señora Honey over at the market bakery."

"Señora Honey is the best!" Isla agreed. "She can whip up just about anything in minutes."

"Come on, the tour's not over yet!" Tora showed Isla the theater room where they'd be watching movies, then the kitchen with boxes of pizza, and the backyard with a fire pit to roast s'mores.

Isla was very impressed.

"There's one more surprise!" Tora sang.

"I sure hope it's another dessert table," Fitz said dreamily.

"She's upstairs in my room." Tora motioned for them to follow.

Isla and Fitz looked at each other. *She?*

CHAPTER 4

PRINCESS ELLA

◊◊◊◊◊◊◊◊◊◊◊◊◊

Isla and Fitz followed Tora to her bedroom.

The Rosas' hallway was lined with lots of family pictures. Tora, of course, was in the center of them all. She really, *really* liked photo shoots.

"I'm excited to see your room for the first time," Isla said. "If it's anything like you, I'm sure it'll be very—"

37

"Behold!" Tora pushed open her bedroom door.

"Pink," Isla finished. Her mouth dropped open.

Stepping into Tora's bedroom was like stepping into the pages of a fairytale book. Strings of twinkling lights hung from the corners of the room. There was a vanity with lots of bows, a table stacked with fashion magazines, and a rack with plenty of poufy dresses.

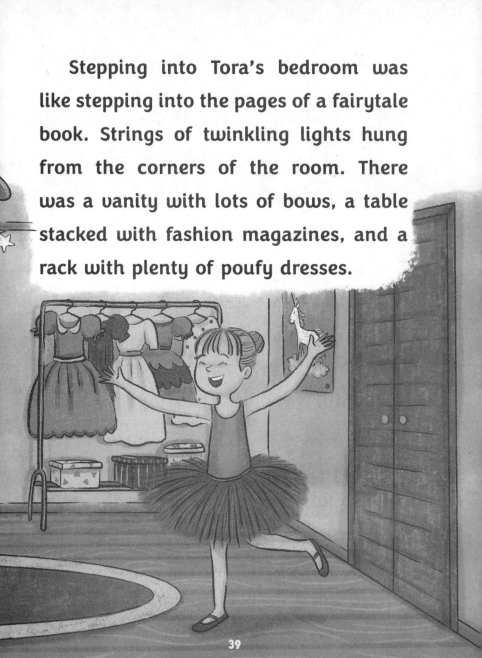

Isla's bedroom smelled like earth, like Sol. Tora's smelled like a rose garden.

"It's like the color pink exploded in here," Fitz whispered.

Suddenly, a flash of purple made Isla jump. "You must be the famous Isla Verde!"

A girl ran out of Tora's large closet and shook Isla's hand excitedly. "I'm Ella Louise Garcia, but you can call me Ella. I was just picking a tiara from Tora's closet. What do you think?"

A gold crown glimmered on her head.

"Very royal," Isla declared. "Nice to meet you, Ella! Or should I say *Princess Ella?*"

Ella nudged Tora on the arm. "Okay, I like her."

Fitz sank back shyly into Isla's curls. "I'll be in here if you need me."

Isla knew what he was thinking. What if Ella thought he was icky, just like Tora had the first time they'd met?

No, Isla thought. A friend of Tora's was a friend of hers. It wasn't fair for Fitz to stay hidden.

"Actually, there's someone else joining the party," Isla said. "Ella, meet my best friend, Fitz."

His head popped out from Isla's curls, and he waved a tiny hand. "Hello."

Isla knew that all the two girls could hear was a *click clack* sound when he talked.

"Your best friend is a gecko?" Ella tilted her head.

Isla and Tora shared a nervous look.

"It's like talking to a dog or kitty," Tora explained. "People do it *all* the time."

But Ella didn't need any convincing at all. "Aww!" she squealed. "Can I hold him?"

Isla looked at Fitz for permission. Fitz nodded, and she happily passed him over into Ella's hands.

"My dads both work at the Sol Island Zoo, and sometimes I get to help out. I feed this one chameleon we've had since he was a little thing." Ella gently petted Fitz.

Isla brightened. "Chameleons are known to be shy, so you must be doing a great job."

"I'm so happy everyone is becoming friends!" Tora twirled in her ballet shoes. Walking on her tippy toes to her vanity, she picked up a jar. "Now let's get this party started with the Activity Jar!"

CHAPTER 5

THE ACTIVITY JAR

◇◆◇◆◇◆◇◆◇◆◇◆◇

The Activity Jar was decorated with lots of stickers and was filled to the brim with small pieces of paper.

The girls sat on the floor with Fitz in the middle.

"The rules are simple," Tora said. "We each pick out an activity and we *have* to do it! No take-backs!"

"No take-backs?" Fitz repeated.

51

"Now that is some real dedication."

"We could do rock, paper, scissors to decide who chooses first," Ella suggested.

They played a few rounds. In the end, Ella won first place, then Isla, Fitz, and finally Tora.

Ella stuck her hand in the jar and plucked out a piece of paper. She turned it over so everyone could see. "Charades! The acting class I took last summer will finally come in handy."

It had been a while since Isla played charades. The last time had been with a group of iguanas on the beach. Ella thought about what she wanted to act out, then raised two fingers.

"Two words!" her friends called out.

Ella spread her arms and started flapping them.

"Oh, oh!" Tora jumped in place. "You're flying!"

Ella nodded. She opened her mouth as she silently sang. What liked to fly a lot and sing at the same time?

"What likes to fly and sing at the same time . . . ?" Fitz wondered out loud.

As Isla was trying to come up with a response, a tiny, barely there voice called out her name. *"Isla!"*

"Huh?" Isla looked around. "Did you say something, Tora?"

Tora frowned. "Nope. I don't think anyone did."

Ella stopped pretend-flying. She joked, "Unless Fitz is suddenly speaking and only you can hear him."

Fitz gulped. "She's on to us!"

Had Isla imagined the voice? "So . . . no one heard that?"

Her friends shook their heads. Isla listened for a moment longer, then shrugged. No voice. No one calling her name.

"Sorry to interrupt your amazing acting, Ella," Isla said, embarrassed.

"Don't be sorry, Isla," Tora said. "This break gave me extra time to think. Were you acting out a robin? Tweedle-lee-dee-dee-dee!"

"Nope!" Ella replied.

Isla was going to throw out her guess, but the quiet voice interrupted again.

"Isla!" it called out. It was so tiny and sounded so far away, Isla wasn't sure if she'd

actually heard anything at all. Still, she jumped to her feet.

"Yes?" she asked, peeking around the room.

Ella looked a bit worried. "Um . . . no one's saying anything, Isla."

"It's Fabio!" Fitz cried out suddenly, hopping into the air.

"No way, it's not that silly singing seagull," Isla replied. Though it wouldn't be surprising if Fabio showed up uninvited.

"Winner, winner!" Ella exclaimed. "You guessed it. I was acting as that terrible singing seagull that lives at the beach."

"That's not . . . ," Isla began. But no one else had heard her name being called. Maybe it was best to leave it alone. "You really *are* a good actress. It was Fitz who guessed!"

Ella looked at the gecko. "Well, however he told you, you're a great team."

Tora stood and fixed her tutu. "Isla, it's your turn to pick something from the jar."

Isla stood to dig for her activity. Pulling out a piece of paper, she unfolded it and showed her friends. "I hope you're ready for . . . scary stories!"

SPOOKY S'MORES

◆◆◆◆◆◆◆◆◆◆◆◆◆◆

In the backyard, Mrs. Rosa passed out plates with marshmallows, chocolate, and crackers. Even Isla's *quesitos* were brought out for a fun Sol twist on s'mores.

Mr. Rosa brought out blankets for the girls to sit on. He also passed out mini flashlights. "I hear we're doing scary stories. You know, back in my day, I was quite the storyteller."

Mrs. Rosa dragged him away. "Honey, I think the girls have it handled."

The girls laughed. Fitz was already scarfing down the *quesitos*.

"Who's ready to get spooked?" Tora asked, pointing a flashlight under her face.

"We are!" Isla said, taking a big bite of her gooey treat.

"Once upon a time," Tora began, "something terrible happened in La Ciudad. . . ."

They all leaned in closer to listen, marshmallow on their faces. La Ciudad, the city where Tora was from, was a total mystery to Isla.

"A girl went to the mall because there was a sale," Tora continued.

"A sale! My favorite." Ella winked at Isla.

Isla agreed. There was nothing better than a yard sale.

"But when she arrived," Tora went on, "ALL THE CUTE CLOTHES WERE SOLD OUT!"

Ella jolted back in surprise. "The horror!"

Tora switched off the flashlight and smiled. "The end!"

Oh. Isla wasn't really spooked, but she went along with it.

Ella took a deep breath. "I'm ready for the next tale of terror."

It was Isla's turn next. Flashlight in hand, she began. "Sol is home to lots of super cool creatures. Imagine my surprise when my Abuelo and I found out that a precious bird species . . . was going *extinct*!"

Gasps echoed through the backyard. But it didn't come from her friends. Behind them, Isla could see a few frogs listening to her story from the backyard bushes. Isla secretly waved at them.

Ella whispered, "I'm not sure what extinct means."

"Extinction means that a whole species disappears from the world," Isla replied. "Sort of like . . . when the cute clothes disappeared forever from the sale."

"Oh boy." Fitz swayed. "This one's getting to me!"

"I never thought about animals disappearing before," Tora said. "That *does* sound scary."

"Luckily, the species bounced back and they're still on the island," Isla said. "So it was only spooky for a moment!"

Ella began to tell her story about a princess losing her tiara.

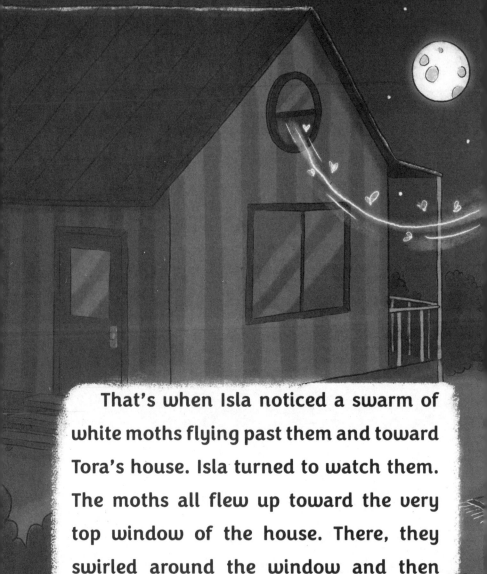

That's when Isla noticed a swarm of white moths flying past them and toward Tora's house. Isla turned to watch them. The moths all flew up toward the very top window of the house. There, they swirled around the window and then the swarm broke apart.

Isla couldn't help but think again about the voice that had called her. Maybe something strange *was* going on.

CHAPTER 7

A CALL
FROM ABOVE

◆◇◆◇◆◇◆◇◆◇◆◇◆

Back in Tora's bedroom, the girls ate a filling dinner of pizza slices.

Though her veggie pizza was delicious, Isla couldn't stop thinking about the moths. "Hey Tora, what's at the very top of your house?" she asked.

"At the top of the house?" Tora echoed. "The roof!"

"I think she's talking about your

attic." Ella laughed. She was trying to keep a face mask from slipping off of her face.

"An attic!" Isla said. "That makes sense."

From what Isla knew about moths, they sure liked attics. But why Tora's?

Tora frowned. "What makes sense?"

Isla wondered for a moment if she should tell her friends about the voice she'd heard earlier. Plus, the moths. . . . But everyone was having such a great time, Isla didn't want to ruin the fun.

"Nothing." Isla decided to go back to her pizza. "Just . . . thinking out loud."

"My dads think out loud a lot," Ella said. "Once, they accidentally told me we were going to a water park for my birthday."

As Isla grabbed a second slice, the tiny voice returned. *"Isla!"*

Even Fitz stopped eating, which was a big deal for the gecko. "Wait . . . did you hear that?"

"You heard it too?" Isla whispered.

"Heard what?" Ella asked. "Are you hearing a voice again, Isla?"

Thunk!

Ella jumped at the sudden sound, mask slipping off. "Whoa! I definitely heard that!"

Isla pointed up. "Whatever it is, it's coming from up there."

"The attic?" Tora asked uneasily. "There's only junk up there."

Thunk, thunk!

"I really hope it's friendly junk," Fitz muttered.

Ella squeaked. "All I know about attics is that they're spooky and haunted!"

Isla handed out the flashlights they'd used outside. "Only one way to find out!"

"Why can't we just go into the kitchen for more snacks instead?" Ella groaned.

Fitz sighed. "If only Isla's adventures were that simple!"

83

CHAPTER 8

STARRY, STARRY GHOST

◆◆◆◆◆◆◆◆◆◆◆◆◆

Isla, Fitz, Tora, and Ella marched up the stairs to the attic.

"You know," Ella whispered, "I was okay with telling scary stories, but I didn't want to be *in* one!"

"Don't worry. It's just a bunch of old stuff up there," Tora said, comforting her friend.

Fitz gulped. "But ghosts love old stuff."

"Come on." Isla led the way. "Everything will be fine!"

Isla had never spoken to ghosts before, but there was a first time for everything. Besides, she might learn something new.

Stepping into the attic, Isla pushed open the door gently. It gave a long creak as it opened.

"If a ghost lives here, they certainly don't believe in cleaning." Tora frowned at all the dust-covered boxes.

Isla stepped closer to a very large spiderweb. "Did you know it can take up to an hour for a spider to build a web?"

"I didn't know that," Ella said. She tried her best to not touch anything. "But I also don't really like spiders."

They walked around the room and found boxes with different labels. One read WINTER CLOTHES. Another was labeled FAMILY PHOTOS.

Tora peeked into the winter clothes box. "I sure miss the colder season. My winter clothes are fabulous!"

Suddenly, Ella pointed her flashlight across the room. "Incoming!"

Isla and Tora pointed their flashlights in the same direction. A large, shadowy figure was just a few steps away . . .

but then Tora laughed. "Ella, that's just
a dress mannequin! I promise the only
scary thing about it is that it hasn't seen
a decent dress in years."

But just as relief washed over Ella, they heard a fluttering sound from somewhere in the room.

"Oh, ghosty ghost," Tora called out quietly. "Come out, come out wherever you are."

Fitz put up his small fists. "Or maybe stay hidden!"

"Wait, I think I see something," Isla said. "There, in the corner of the ceiling!"

Together, the girls slowly lifted their flashlights to the top corner of the attic and pointed them directly at a spiderweb. Suddenly, something fluttered right toward them.

STUCK
IN A WEB

◆◆◆◆◆◆◆◆◆◆◆◆◆◆

"What is that?" Ella shrieked, ducking.

But the fluttering thing never actually reached them. Isla pointed her flashlight at it again and gasped. It wasn't a spider or a ghost.

"It's a moth!" Isla said.

A large moth tried to flap his wings, but the sticky web held him back no matter how hard he fought.

His wings were so big, they made a *thunk* when they hit the wall.

"Thank goodness you're here," the moth cried out in a tiny voice. "I thought you'd never hear me!"

"This all makes sense now," Fitz said, relieved. "The voice calling you, the thunk, thunk, thunks."

Tora wrinkled her nose. "Moths make me a little nervous. They're like scary butterflies."

The moth fluttered his wings in a way that showed he was upset. "Hey! Butterflies are the scary ones!"

Isla smiled. "If you look closely, you'll see they also have pretty wings. Look at the blue color and little white dots."

Tora and Ella stepped closer.

"Huh, you're right," Ella said. "Its wings kinda look like a starry night."

Fitz tapped Isla on her shoulder. "Uh, should we help him get out of there?"

She almost asked the moth a question, but remembered that Ella was still beside her. While Tora already knew her secret, Isla's new friend did not.

Tora caught on quickly, winking at Isla. "Ella, do you want to help me grab a stepping stool? We'll be back in a few minutes, Isla."

As soon as the friends left, Isla turned back to the moth. "I'll get you out of there, little one. I'm Isla Verde. What's your name?"

"Of course you're Isla Verde," the moth said. "I knew it the second I heard your voice."

"You know who I am?" Isla couldn't help but feel a little flattered.

"Everyone knows who you are!" the moth exclaimed. "You helped my sister when she was stuck in your Abuelo's attic. We're always getting stuck in attics."

"No kidding!" Fitz said. "How come you guys fly up here so much?"

The moth sighed dreamily. "It's the best place to admire the moon."

The moth, Fitz, and Isla turned to look at a small window in the attic. Moonlight streamed in gently. It made Isla feel as if she was in a magical world. Though her island home always felt magical.

Isla understood the moth perfectly. "The moon is a rare beauty."

"I was enjoying the view so much that I didn't watch where I was flying," the moth continued. "Now I'm in this sticky situation. I had hoped the spider who lives here could help me out, but I don't think anyone's home."

Fitz shivered. "Last time I tried to be nice to a spider, she yelled at me for stepping on her web. Can you believe that?"

"To be fair, that spider had worked really hard on her web," Isla pointed out to him.

Fitz blushed. "It was an accident!"

Moments later, Tora and Ella returned with a stepping stool. "Here you go, Isla!"

"Thank you." Carefully, Isla stepped on to the highest step, and she began to pull the moth's wings free. "You're stuck in there good, aren't you? Don't you worry, I got you . . . almost there . . . and done!"

"Freedom!" the moth cried out. He fluttered around in happy circles. "Oh, thank you, thank you so very much! I don't know what I would have done if you hadn't come."

"Whoa!" Tora gasped. "It really *is* pretty!"

"Nice job, Isla," Ella cheered, giving Isla a high five.

Isla beamed. "It was a group effort."

"Wait!" Fitz yelped. "We didn't get your name!"

"Luna!" the moth replied. "Fitting, don't you think?"

Isla smiled as she watched Luna fly out the open attic window and deep into the night.

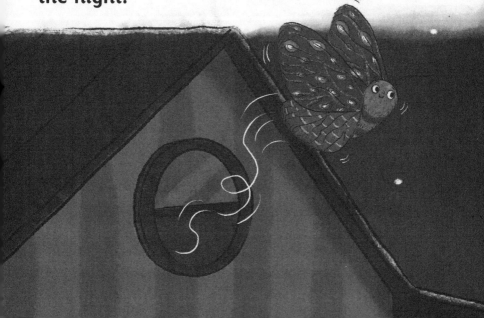

CHAPTER 10

BEST SLEEPOVER EVER

◊◊◊◊◊◊◊◊◊◊◊◊◊

Back in Tora's room, the girls slipped into their sleeping bags.

"Well, this sleepover will be very hard to forget!" Ella laughed. "I don't know when I'll get the chance to speak to a moth again."

Isla agreed. "No one throws a party like Tora."

Tora winked.

Ella twirled her hands. "I'm sorry we didn't believe you before."

"Don't worry about it," Isla said. "It's not always easy when you're listening to something new."

The sound of snoring made Isla look down at her lap. Fitz was belly-up with his mouth open. The girls laughed.

"Well, I definitely heard that," Tora said. "I think Fitz has the right idea!"

As the girls got ready for bed, Isla thought about her new moth friend. Yawning, she said, "I hope Luna finds a nice new attic without too many spiderwebs."

"Luna?" Ella raised her eyebrows.

"Is that what you named the moth?" Tora asked, trying to help Isla out.

"I didn't really name it," Isla admitted. "I just learned that if you listen with your whole heart, you'll hear what anyone has to say."

"Oh, I like that," Ella said. "I'll have to listen harder when I'm helping my dads at the zoo. Ugh, sometimes that chameleon gives me such a stink eye!"

"Maybe we could go to the zoo together one day," Isla offered. "I'm happy to help you figure it out."

Isla hoped that no matter what, she would always be around to help spread a little love on Sol. Even in attics with ghosts—or moths.

DON'T MISS ISLA'S NEXT ADVENTURE!

HERE'S A SNEAK PEEK!

◇◇◇◇◇◇◇◇◇◇◇◇◇◇

The sweet, mouthwatering scent of cinnamon muffins wrapped itself around Isla Verde.

She eagerly watched them through the oven door as they slowly rose.

Fitz, Isla's gecko best friend, sighed happily as he sat on her shoulder. Just as Isla loved everything about her home in Sol, Fitz loved everything to do with food. Especially Abuela's baking.

Living right next door to Isla's

grandparents was an added bonus.

"This oven is my new best friend," Fitz said dreamily. "Wow . . . look how it bakes."

Isla laughed. "Are you replacing me with an oven?"

"Jeez, can you blame me? This thing is a baking machine," Fitz joked. "And it smells a-ma-zing."

"Now you're just saying I'm stinky." Isla lifted a curl and sniffed. "Maybe my new shampoo isn't strong enough. The rain forest frogs made it from river water."

Fitz stuck his tongue out. *"That* explains it!"

From squeaky clean counters to

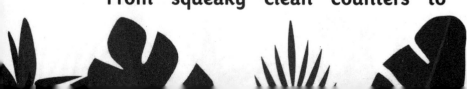

the latest model blender, everything in Abuela's kitchen was the best of the best. She was a cookbook writer, so it made sense she had an oven even a gecko loved.

It was also no wonder Abuela had won the annual Sol Bake-Off so many times. Abuelo had even built a special shelf to place the five glittering Golden Spoon trophies.

Click!

Broken out of her sugary trance, Isla turned to see her grandparents coming in from the backyard.

"Hola, hola!" Abuela said. She undid the big bow in front of her apron, slipped it off, and folded it over a chair.

Like Mama, Abuela could often be found wearing a stained apron. Mama's was usually covered with soil and Abuela's with flour.

"The berries for tomorrow are here!" Fitz cheered. "Come on!"

Isla stood up and skipped to the table.

"How was it? Did you pick enough raspberries? Did you?" she asked in a rush. When she was excited, Isla spoke as quickly as a hummingbird flew. "I just *know* you'll win the Golden Spoon again, Abuela!"

Her grandparents shared a look that made Isla pause. It was the kind of expression Fitz had when he ran out of banana slices to eat. Not very good.